Ghosts
Don't Eat
Potato Chips

Ghosts Don't Eat Potato Chips

by Debbie Dadey
and
Marcia Thornton Jones

illustrated by John Steven Gurney

A
LITTLE APPLE
PAPERBACK

SCHOLASTIC INC.

New York Toronto London Auckland Sydney

ISBN 0-590-45854-X

Copyright © 1992 by Debby Dadey and Marcia Thornton Jones.
Illustrations copyright © 1992 by Scholastic Inc.
All rights reserved. Published by Scholastic Inc.
APPLE PAPERBACKS is a registered trademark of Scholastic Inc.

12 11 10 9   4 5 6 7/9

Printed in the U.S.A.   40

First Scholastic printing, September 1992

For three great brothers:
Randall J. Thornton
Frank L. Gibson
David W. Gibson

Contents

1

Great-aunt Mathilda

"Aw, Grandma," Eddie whined. "Why do I have to go? Great-aunt Mathilda doesn't even like me."

Eddie's grandmother sighed. "Because Mathilda is my sister, and families take care of each other."

"That old bat never did anything for us," Eddie mumbled.

Eddie's grandmother thumped him on the head. "That's not the point! She's been by herself since Uncle Jasper died. Now she's sick and needs our help. All you have to do is take her meals to her. You and Howie can take her lunch on your way to the playground."

Eddie pulled a baseball cap over his curly red hair and grabbed the dish off the kitchen counter. He didn't complain

to his grandmother again, but he slammed the door extra hard on his way out.

His best friend, Howie, was waiting for him at the street corner. "What's that?" Howie asked.

"It's a sick casserole for my Great-aunt Mathilda."

"Don't you mean it's a great casserole for your sick aunt?" Howie asked.

Eddie snickered. "You don't know my grandmother's cooking!"

Howie laughed and pulled out a crushed

bag of potato chips from his shirt pocket. "You want some garlic chips?"

"No! Those chips are worse than my grandmother's cooking!" Eddie said. "You should get the kind I like."

The two boys headed down a side street with Howie crunching away. In just a few minutes they stood in front of Aunt Mathilda's house.

The branches of a huge weeping willow tree dragged the ground beside the fence. The rusty iron gate squeaked open. Eddie and Howie looked at the big house without saying a word. Dark windows stared down at them as they walked up the crumbling steps to the door.

"This house looks like a reject from an old horror movie," Howie whispered.

Eddie nodded. "It's definitely ready for a wrecking ball."

Howie crunched nervously on his potato chips. "Let's hurry up, this place is creepy!"

Eddie lifted the rusting door knocker and then let it fall with a thud. A window on the second floor creaked open, and a gray-haired woman looked out. "Who's at my door?"

"It's us," Eddie yelled. "Grandma sent your lunch."

Aunt Mathilda wrinkled her nose like she'd just sucked a lemon. "Well, hurry and bring it to me. And shut the door behind you!" Then she slammed the window so hard, it rattled.

Eddie pushed the door open. A musty smell hit them like an ocean wave.

"Phew. It smells like something died in here. Hasn't your Aunt Mathilda ever heard of air fresheners?" Howie asked.

"Old people don't care when things stink," Eddie said.

"Quit that whispering and bring me my lunch," Aunt Mathilda said from her bedroom. "An old lady could die of starvation before getting fed by you."

"I'd like to feed her a thing or two," Eddie muttered. "Only it wouldn't be supper!"

The two kids stepped around a pile of yellowed newspapers and started up the creaking steps. Eddie's shoelaces slapped the faded carpet, and the boys sidestepped a broken chair in the upstairs hall. Aunt Mathilda's room was at the end of the hall on the second floor.

Aunt Mathilda was sitting up in bed with a box of tissues by her side. Wadded-up tissues were scattered on the floor. Wisps of gray hair hung around her face like spiderwebs, and her wrinkled skin was the color of old pears. She looked like she had been through World War Two instead of the flu. She pointed a bony finger at Eddie. "I remember you. You're the mean one!"

Eddie shrugged. "It must run in the family."

"Hummph," Aunt Mathilda grunted. "Who's that with you? I don't know him."

Howie choked on a potato chip. "I'm Eddie's friend, Howie. Would you like some chips?" He held out the crumpled bag.

"That's the garlic kind my Jasper always ate. It's probably what killed him."

"Who's Jasper?" Howie whispered as he stuffed the bag into his shirt pocket.

"My dead uncle," Eddie whispered back. Then, before Aunt Mathilda could say anything else, Eddie shoved the dish at her. "Grandma said to ask if you needed anything else."

Aunt Mathilda nodded. "As long as you're here, you can water the garden."

As they walked down the steps, Eddie and Howie heard Aunt Mathilda blowing her nose.

"I never knew you had a crazy aunt," Howie said.

"She's not half as crazy as Uncle Jasper was," Eddie said as he pushed open the back door. "We're just lucky he's not around anymore!"

2

Weed Soup

"I can't believe she calls this a garden," Eddie said, shaking his head. "It's just a bunch of weeds."

"I bet your Aunt Mathilda uses it to make weed soup." Howie laughed as he helped drag a garden hose between the gnarled trees.

"Crabgrass salad, too," Eddie giggled as he tried to turn on the water. "Something's wrong with this faucet."

"Let me try," Howie said, dropping his bag of potato chips on an old picnic table.

"No. If I can't get it, you sure can't." Eddie didn't get a chance to try again because Aunt Mathilda's screech interrupted them.

"Did you expect me to eat this with my

fingers?" she yelled from the window. "Bring me a fork and a glass of water."

Eddie shoved the hose at Howie. "You'll have to water the garden while I go water Aunt Mathilda."

Howie looked at the old house as his friend disappeared inside. Several windows were broken, and wood was nailed over the empty spaces. The attic window was so high, Howie had to tilt his head back to see it.

What Howie saw made him freeze. Someone was staring down from the attic window. Howie rubbed his eyes and looked again. No one was there.

"That's strange," Howie muttered.

"You're strange," Eddie said as he came out the back door. "If you don't watch out a bird will get you in the eye."

Howie ignored Eddie's remark. "Were you just in the attic?"

Eddie grabbed the hose from Howie. "I don't even know how to get to the attic of this joint."

"Does anyone else live here?" Howie asked.

"Just my crazy aunt." Eddie tried to twist the water spigot. "Why do you care?"

"Maybe we'd better call the police because I just saw someone in the attic." Howie pointed to the small window at the top of the house.

Eddie stared at the window for a few minutes and then laughed. "Don't be silly, it was just a shadow from those big trees."

Howie looked at the window again. But he didn't see anything because Eddie finally got the hose on and squirted Howie right in the face.

"Cut it out," Howie yelled.

Eddie laughed. "I thought you might like to cool off."

Howie backed away from the weed patch. "If you don't quit it, I'm going to the playground without you."

"Okay, I'll stop if you'll wait for me." As Eddie squirted the plants, Howie went to get his potato chips. Instead, he found an empty chip bag. "Who said you could eat all my chips?"

"I told you, I hate garlic chips," Eddie said.

Howie looked under the old picnic table and gulped. "Eddie, come here."

Eddie dropped the hose and walked over to the picnic table. "What do you want?" he asked.

Howie pointed. "Look under there."

Eddie shook his head, but he glanced

under the table. "So, you spilled your chips. What's the big deal?"

Howie banged his hand on the table. "Look, Eddie. Really look. This is important."

"Okay, okay. Keep your eyeballs glued on." Eddie looked again. "Hey, the chips are letters. A . . . T . . . T . . . I . . . C. What's that spell?"

"ATTIC!" Howie yelled at Eddie. "Somebody spelled out attic."

Eddie shrugged. "It's just a coincidence. Either that or Aunt Mathilda has smart ants in her yard." With that, Eddie stepped on the chips and smashed them to tiny pieces.

Howie looked back up at the attic window. It was still empty. Maybe it had been a shadow. But what if it hadn't?

3

Smarty-Pants

Eddie caught up with Howie at the oak tree on the playground. The giant tree made a perfect Saturday morning meeting place for the kids from Bailey Elementary School. Two other third-graders, Liza and Melody, were waiting for them.

Liza giggled and pushed back her blonde hair. "What happened to you?"

"It looks like you've been slimed by the Loch Ness Monster," Melody said.

Howie squeezed his T-shirt and water oozed into his tennis shoe. "Hosehead tried to squirt me into the next county."

"I was just trying to cool you off," Eddie told him. "After all, you were so hot you were seeing things."

"What's he talking about?" Melody asked.

Howie shook his wet head and splattered water on his friends. "I saw someone looking out his crazy aunt's window."

"He also saw potato chips so smart they could win a spelling bee." Eddie laughed.

Howie's face turned red. "Maybe the chips were a coincidence, but there really was somebody in the attic."

"It was probably Eddie's aunt," Melody told Howie.

"No, she's sick in bed," Howie said. "*And* she lives all by herself."

Liza touched Eddie on his shoulder. "I didn't know your sweet aunt was sick."

"There's nothing sweet about that old bat," Eddie snickered.

"Eddie! You shouldn't talk about sick people like that," Liza said.

"You guys are missing the point," Howie interrupted. "What if there really is somebody hiding up in that attic?"

"No one's up there except in your loony imagination," Eddie laughed. "I told you, it was just the tree's shadow."

"It couldn't be a shadow," Melody told them.

"How do you know that, Miss Smarty-Pants?" Eddie asked. "You weren't there."

"It's been cloudy all day," Melody snapped. "You can't have shadows without sun!"

Howie pointed a finger at Eddie. "She's right."

"Maybe you better call the police," Liza said.

"Police don't chase shadows." Eddie laughed.

"But there could be a crazy lunatic just waiting for the chance to rob your aunt," said Howie.

Eddie shook his head. "Nobody would want to rob my aunt. She's so poor she can't even afford to fix up her house."

"Still, wouldn't you feel terrible if something happened to your aunt and you didn't help her?" Liza asked.

Howie nodded. "At least tell her."

"But we just got here," Eddie snapped. "We'll tell her later."

"Stop thinking about yourself," Liza said. "You better warn her now before something awful happens."

"Something awful *has* happened," Eddie said. "I listened to my silly friends. If you goody-goodies are so worried about Aunt Mathilda, you can go with me. Meet me at her house at seven o'clock when I take supper to her. And don't be late."

His friends watched Eddie stomp away from the tree toward some boys playing softball. "Are you sure there was someone at that window?" Melody asked Howie.

"I know what I saw," Howie said slowly. "And it was no shadow."

4

The Legend

At seven o'clock, Eddie, Howie, Liza, and Melody stared up at the attic window. Liza's eyes were big and round. "You didn't tell me your aunt lives in a haunted house."

"You're as bad as Howie," Eddie told her. "Next, you'll be seeing things, too."

"Don't you know the legend behind this house?" Liza asked. "Three years ago, weird things started happening at all hours of the night. Strange lights and funny noises came from the attic."

"What kind of noises?" Melody asked.

"Ghostly footsteps," Liza said seriously, "and whistling."

"That's all stupid nonsense," Eddie interrupted.

"It is not," Liza snapped. "My dad told

me that ghosts can't rest if something they did during their lives is causing loved ones to suffer. They're doomed to wander until someone rights the wrong for them."

Eddie shook his head and pushed open the squeaky gate. "Then you'll never rest because you're always making me suffer."

"But maybe that's what Howie saw," Liza said firmly.

"What?" Melody asked.

"A ghost," Liza whispered.

"And maybe your head is full of Rice Krispies!" Eddie muttered to himself as he headed up the sidewalk. "My aunt may be crazy," Eddie told them on the porch, "but she's no ghost."

"How can you be sure?" Melody asked.

"Because you have to be dead to be a ghost, and Great-aunt Mathilda is too mean to die," Eddie joked as he banged on the front door.

Just like before, the second floor window creaked open and Aunt Mathilda peered down at them. "Quit that racket. How's a sick woman supposed to get any rest with you pounding on the door?"

Eddie held up his grandmother's casserole dish. "Should I just throw this in the trash?"

"What? And let me starve?" Aunt Mathilda snapped. "Bring it up here and don't be all day about it."

"I told you she was crazy," Howie whispered to Liza as they went in the house.

"She's not crazy," Liza said. "She's just cranky because she doesn't feel well."

"Then she hasn't felt well since 1942," Eddie said as he led them to his aunt's bedroom.

Aunt Mathilda was still in bed. Her covers looked like a warthog had been rooting in them, and the mound of used tissues on the floor had grown a foot. Aunt Mathilda reached out her hands for

the casserole dish and fork. "How many kids does it take to bring an old woman dinner?"

Liza smiled. "My name is Liza, and this is Melody. It's nice to meet you."

"Hummph," Aunt Mathilda said as she dug into her dinner.

"We came to tell you something," Melody added. But she never got the chance because Aunt Mathilda took a big bite of casserole and spit it out all over the bed.

"I can't eat this. It's as cold as a park bench in February. You'll have to heat it up in the oven."

"We'd be happy to," Liza chirped as she picked up the cold dish. Her three friends followed her out of the room.

Aunt Mathilda called after them, "Come back up here while it's heating so I can keep an eye on you."

The kids hurried to the kitchen. "I've got better things to do than play nursemaid to an old grouch," Eddie complained.

"Now, Eddie. You shouldn't talk about your great-aunt that way. It won't take long to heat this up, then we can tell her about the attic," Liza said.

"How do you work this stove anyway?" Melody asked.

"Do I look like Betty Crocker? I've never used an oven in my life," Eddie admitted.

"Me neither," Howie said.

Eddie twirled the knob. "My grandmother does it all the time so it can't be that hard."

Liza stuck the casserole in the oven, and they went back upstairs. They were in the upstairs hall when they heard it.

THUMP.

"Listen," Howie hissed. The four kids stood in the middle of the dusty hallway. "It sounds like something fell over in the attic."

THUMP. THUMP. THUMP.

"It sounds like footsteps to me," Melody whispered. "Somebody *is* up there."

"Or else it's the ghost," Liza gulped as she started backing down the hall.

Melody grabbed Liza's arm. "We've got to warn Aunt Mathilda."

"Calm down," Eddie laughed. "It's probably just rats."

"I've never heard rats whistle," Howie said hoarsely as a high-pitched melody floated down from above.

5

Up in Smoke

"Did you hear that?" Liza asked as they burst into the bedroom.

Aunt Mathilda was busy shuffling a deck of cards like a professional card-shark. "Hear what?" she asked.

"It sounds like someone is in the attic," Melody told her. "We heard footsteps and whistling."

Aunt Mathilda shrugged. "There're always creaks in an old house like this."

"But this afternoon I saw a face in the attic window," Howie said. "Maybe we should take a look around upstairs — just to be sure."

"Hummph. Nobody's going up in that attic," Aunt Mathilda said firmly. "Jasper was the only one who ever went up there.

It's been three years since he died and that creaky floor's probably not safe anymore."

"Are you sure it's just old floorboards?" Liza asked.

"Of course," Aunt Mathilda snapped. "Now, I've had enough of your silly talk. I want to play cards."

The four kids looked at each other and shrugged. If Aunt Mathilda wasn't worried, maybe they shouldn't be either. Liza clapped her hands. "Oh, I just love to play Go Fish."

"Fish!" Aunt Mathilda bellowed. "I was thinking more about poker."

"Now, you're talking." Eddie smiled.

The kids stared because Aunt Mathilda dealt the cards with the speed of a machine gun. It wasn't long before the five of them were playing Black Jack and Three-card Monte.

"How'd an old lady like you learn to be such a good poker player?" Melody asked

after Aunt Mathilda had won another game.

"That's one good thing about being old! I know a lot more than little snots like you." Aunt Mathilda laughed.

Liza giggled along with her. Eddie even laughed as he grabbed the cards to deal a new game.

Howie sniffed the air. "Do you smell something funny?"

"The casserole," Melody gasped.

"You're burning down my house," Aunt Mathilda screamed as the kids rushed out of the room.

The kitchen was filled with so much smoke that none of the kids noticed the dark shadow by the refrigerator.

"Turn off the oven," Eddie hollered, grabbing a potholder.

Melody reached for the dial and froze. "It *is* off!"

"Right, this burned all by itself," Eddie snapped, opening the oven door. Black smoke billowed out and Liza coughed. Eddie dropped the crispy casserole into the kitchen sink.

"Oh, no," Melody choked when she saw the black mess.

"There's no way your Aunt Mathilda will eat this," Howie said, holding his nose.

Liza took an old dish towel and started fanning the smoke. "We can't let her starve to death."

Aunt Mathilda screamed from the top of the stairs, "What're you ruffians trying to do? Cook me alive?"

Eddie looked at Liza. "Maybe we *should* let her starve."

"I like your aunt. After all, she did teach us to play poker," Melody said.

"We've got to tell her what happened," Howie said.

"Tell me what?" Aunt Mathilda snapped as she shuffled into the kitchen.

Liza reached out for Aunt Mathilda's arm. "You shouldn't be out of bed!"

"I couldn't let you barbecue me," Aunt Mathilda coughed. "I suppose you've ruined my supper," she said.

"Well," Eddie stammered. "It did get a little well done."

"Smells to me like it burned to kingdom come," Aunt Mathilda wheezed as she pulled an ancient black coin purse from her robe pocket. "Eddie, you'll have to clean this up. And open the windows to let all that smoke out! The rest of you can get my supper. I guess I'll have to pay for it. You kids must think I'm made of money."

Aunt Mathilda dug into the coin purse with her long bony fingers. Slowly, she pulled out several crumpled bills.

"I'd better give you money to buy something. If I don't you'll eat mine before you get back here."

"We wouldn't do that," Liza insisted.

"Hummph," Aunt Mathilda snorted. "Make sure you don't. Hurry to that fast food joint around the corner."

"You mean Burger Doodle?" Melody asked.

Aunt Mathilda nodded. "That's the one. Jasper loved their Double Onion Doodle Burgers and those garlic chips. Pick me up some and get something for yourselves."

"We'll be glad to get your dinner," Liza said. "But you'd better get back to bed before you start coughing again!"

"Hummph," Aunt Mathilda said as she left the room. "Just don't take all day to do it."

Eddie walked with his friends to the front door. "Will you clean up the kitchen for me?" Eddie said to Melody.

"She's your aunt," Melody smiled as she opened the door. "You clean it up. But we'll bring you back a Doodlegum Shake."

"Bring me three," Eddie ordered.

"Quit being so greedy," Liza told him.

"Well, make it fast or she'll have us running errands all night."

"She's not that bad," Liza said.

"My aunt is as rotten as those Double Onion Doodle Burgers," Eddie said. "Aunt Mathilda and Uncle Jasper are the only people I've ever known who actually ate them."

Melody giggled. "But those Doodlegum Shakes are the best in town."

"And I like the garlic chips," Howie yelled as he started running. "Last one there is a slimy Doodle Burger."

Eddie watched his friends race down the street. He closed the door and went back to the kitchen. When he got there, the casserole dish was already sparkling clean and the windows were wide open.

6

Double Onion Doodle Burgers and Garlic Potato Chips

Howie opened a new bag of garlic chips as the three kids opened the rusty gate in front of Aunt Mathilda's house. "Phew. Those Double Onion Doodle Burgers stink."

Melody held up the greasy paper bag. "You're right, you can smell these three miles away."

Liza held her nose and ran away from the burgers. "Get those away from me!"

But Melody couldn't resist teasing Liza a little bit. She chased her around the house.

Howie was still in the front yard munching his chips when he heard Melody

36

scream. When he got to the backyard, Melody was face down on the ground. "What happened?" he asked.

Melody lifted her face out of the grass. "I tripped over a stupid tree root," she said.

Howie grabbed an arm to pull her up. "Are you okay?"

"I'm all right." Melody sat up. "But I'm afraid these Doodle Burgers are squished.

They're flatter than a rattlesnake run over by a two-ton semi-truck."

"We'll have to fluff them up a little," Liza said.

"They're hamburgers," Melody said, "not pillows."

They didn't see the dark shadow as Howie picked up the smashed bag and headed inside.

"If anybody can fix these burgers, I can," he said as he dumped the garlic chips on the kitchen table. Then he put the burgers onto a cracked plate and patted them with his hands.

"Maybe she won't notice," Liza suggested.

"If you ask me," Howie told them with a grin, "they look better than they usually do."

"What's taking you guys so long?" Eddie asked as he clomped down the stairs. "Aunt Mathilda is starving, and I'm tired of getting beat at poker. By the way, you really had me tricked. I just can't figure out when you did it."

"What are you talking about?" Howie asked.

"When you cleaned up the casserole catastrophe," Eddie said.

His three friends glanced at each other. "We didn't touch that mess," Melody said slowly.

"Well, if you didn't clean it up, and I didn't clean it up, then who did?" Eddie asked as he turned and grabbed the plate off the counter. "Hey! Who bit the burger?"

His three friends stared at the half-eaten burger. "Not me," they all said at once.

"Look! Someone's been eating the garlic chips, too," Melody said.

"And they're all over the floor," Liza said. "What will we tell Aunt Mathilda?"

"No problem," Eddie said. "We'll just

put them back on the plate. Aunt Mathilda will never know."

The four kids picked up the chips that were scattered on the kitchen floor. "There's more out in the hall," Melody said.

"It's a garlic chip trail," Howie said quietly.

The trail led them to an open door at the top of the stairs. A cold draft made Liza shiver. "That must be the attic. It's as if someone's trying to lead us up there."

"With potato chips?" Eddie laughed.

"How did the door get opened?" Melody whispered. "I'm sure it wasn't open before."

Eddie didn't have time to answer.

"I'm going to call the police if you don't bring me some food. I'm about to pass out from hunger up here," Aunt Mathilda screamed from her room.

"She sounds to me like she has plenty

of strength left," Eddie muttered. He closed the attic door and stomped into Aunt Mathilda's room with his three friends following.

Aunt Mathilda grabbed the plate and started wolfing down a slimy Doodle Burger. Grease from the burger oozed down her bony fingers.

"That's so disgusting," Melody whispered.

"At least she didn't notice they were squished," Liza whispered back.

But Howie did notice something — a picture on Great-aunt Mathilda's nightstand.

"Look at the man in that picture," Howie said softly to Eddie. "That's the man in the attic window."

Eddie looked at the picture. "Don't be silly. That's my uncle Jasper. And he's dead."

7

Uncle Jasper?

"It's true," Howie told his friends. "The man in the window looks just like Uncle Jasper. He was even wearing the same hat." The four kids were under the oak tree. Thick storm clouds hung low in the sky.

"What a strange coincidence," Melody said.

"What's really weird is that Jasper liked Doodle Burgers," Liza pointed out. "And somebody took a bite out of one of ours."

"And someone nibbled on my garlic potato chips," Howie added.

Eddie laughed. "And my aunt thought only Uncle Jasper liked garlic chips and Doodle Burgers."

"If I didn't know better," Liza said, "I'd

say Jasper *is* a ghost, and he's living in the attic!"

Her three friends stared at her for a second before they burst into a fit of giggles.

"And Aunt Mathilda's really Joan of Arc," Eddie snickered.

Liza got mad. "This is nothing to laugh about."

"You have to admit," Melody said slowly, "it is sort of spooky."

Howie nodded. "After all, somebody did spell out the word 'attic' with my garlic chips."

"Big deal," Eddie said. "It doesn't take a college degree to spell."

"Well, explain the trail of garlic chips leading to the attic, and the footsteps we heard up there," Melody demanded.

Eddie fell on the ground laughing. "You guys have sawdust for brains. You've been reading too many ghost stories."

"Ghosts are white and float through walls," Howie added.

"Yeah," Eddie laughed. "And they definitely don't eat potato chips."

Melody put her hands on her hips. "If you're so sure, you'll go up in the attic and prove there's no ghost."

"But Aunt Mathilda said the attic's not safe," Liza said.

"Nothing can stop me from going up there," Eddie bragged. "Not even Aunt Mathilda."

8

Ghost Hunt

"Why do we have to go tonight?" Melody asked. The four kids were standing in front of Aunt Mathilda's house. The wind was blowing the leaves, causing a strange rustling sound.

"We have to go when she's asleep, don't we?" Eddie swung the gate open. "We're here. Let's get it over with."

"I can't believe we're actually going ghost hunting," Howie shivered.

"There *is* no ghost," Eddie said.

"Ghost, or no ghost, I don't see anything," Melody whispered. "How do we find a ghost?"

"Let's call him," Liza suggested.

"He's not a dog," Eddie snapped.

"How else do you plan on finding him?" Liza asked.

. Eddie shrugged his shoulders. Then they all started whispering into the darkness. "Jasper! Jasper!"

"Shhh," Melody hissed. "I think I hear something."

They all strained to hear.

"Ohhhh. . .Ohhhh."

"My gosh," Liza screeched. "It's Uncle Jasper's ghost."

"It's coming from inside the house," Melody whispered.

"Ohhhh . . . Ohhhh," they heard again.

"We've got to go in there and find what's making that noise," Eddie said bravely.

"Not me," Liza and Melody said together.

"What about Aunt Mathilda? We can't leave her in there with a ghost!" Howie reminded them.

"You're right," Liza nodded. "Poor Aunt Mathilda. She's probably scared to death."

"My Great-aunt Mathilda isn't scared of anything," Eddie bragged.

"Ohhhh . . . Ohhhh," they heard again.

"Come on," Eddie said, and he pushed open the front door. His three friends followed closely behind him.

"Your aunt should lock her door," Melody said. "Anybody could just walk in."

"Anybody just did," Eddie snickered.

"Listen," Liza whispered. "I hear whistling."

"It's just the wind blowing through cracks," Eddie said.

"I've never heard the wind whistle 'Yankee Doodle' before," Howie muttered.

It was true. Someone was whistling the lively tune. "It must be Aunt Mathilda," Eddie said. But when they reached her bedroom, the entire house was deathly still.

"Aunt Mathilda?" Eddie whispered outside her bedroom door. "It's me, Eddie. Are you okay?"

There was no answer.

"Maybe she's asleep," Howie said.

"Maybe the ghost got her," Liza suggested.

"You better go in and check on her," Melody said quietly.

"I'm not going in there," Eddie said. "She could be in her underwear!"

"She's your aunt." Liza shook her finger at Eddie. "You have to go in there."

"You're all chickens," Eddie accused.

"Am not," Melody snapped.

Eddie grabbed Melody's arm. "Then prove it! Go with me."

Slowly, he turned the knob, and the door groaned open.

9

Yankee Doodle

Aunt Mathilda was sprawled across the rumpled bed. Her face was white as a ghost.

"Is she d-d-dead?" Melody whispered.

Before Eddie could answer Aunt Mathilda slowly opened her bloodshot eyes. "Of course I'm not dead," she wheezed.

Eddie snickered, "She's too mean to die!"

Liza touched his arm and said softly, "She looks pretty sick to me."

Aunt Mathilda grabbed her chest as she broke into a coughing fit. "Jasper," Aunt Mathilda gasped. "Get in here. I need you."

"She's finally done it," Eddie said. "She's gone completely bonkers."

"Jasper," Aunt Mathilda called again.

Eddie touched his aunt's hand. "Uncle Jasper is dead and gone."

"No, he's not." Aunt Mathilda coughed and pointed to the door. "I hear him."

"All I hear is somebody whistling 'Yankee Doodle'," Howie said softly.

Aunt Mathilda nodded. "That's him! That's my Jasper!"

"I think she's had one Double Onion Doodle Burger too many," Eddie mumbled.

"I think you need to call her doctor," Melody said.

"NO!" Aunt Mathilda screamed. "I can't afford a doctor."

"You have to go to the doctor," Eddie said. "You're sick. Besides, Grandma says you have plenty of money."

Aunt Mathilda shook her head. "That's why you have to get Jasper. He has all the money. If you won't get him, then I will." Aunt Mathilda threw back the covers and stuck out her skinny legs.

"She's delirious," Eddie told his friends. "I'm calling 911. You keep her in bed."

His friends could hear Eddie racing down the steps to the phone in the kitchen. Melody grabbed Aunt Mathilda around her waist and wrestled her back into bed. "Hurry," Melody screamed as she threw the covers back on the old woman. "Your aunt is burning up with fever. We've got to get her to the hospital."

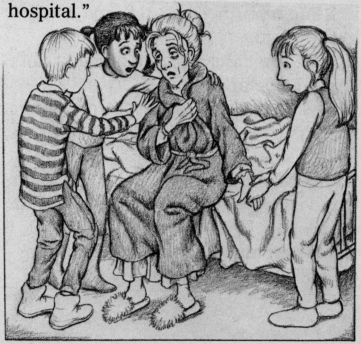

"But I'm too poor to go to the hospital," Aunt Mathilda wailed. It took all the kids to hold Aunt Mathilda in bed until the ambulance came.

"Put me down," she yelled as the medics slid her into the back of the ambulance. "I don't want to go to the hospital."

When the tall medic patted her hand, Aunt Mathilda tried to bite him. "I said, put me down," she told him. "I can't afford hospitals."

As he climbed into the ambulance, the medic glanced at Eddie. "Your aunt will be fine. But she better be able to find a way to pay. Hospitals aren't cheap, you know."

Eddie looked him in the eye. "Don't worry. She'll pay."

Lightning cracked the sky, and thunder rumbled in the distance as the ambulance sped away.

"But Aunt Mathilda doesn't have money," Liza said softly.

"Maybe Eddie's grandmother will help," Howie said. "Right now, we better make sure all the windows are closed, and get home. I think those clouds are ready to dump a billion gallons of rain."

Melody shivered and looked at the thick clouds. Then she glanced at the old house. "Look!" she screamed. "Look in the attic window."

Her three friends glanced up just in time to see the shadow of a man wearing a hat.

"Oh my gosh," Liza screamed. "It's the ghost!"

trunk. "Hey, that looks like the box we saw in our teacher's basement," Eddie remembered.

"It does," Melody agreed. "We thought it was a vampire's coffin."

Eddie nodded to the trunk. "This one's long enough for a vampire, too. Do you think Aunt Mathilda keeps vampires in her attic?"

"Shhh. Listen," Melody hissed. "I think I *do* hear something inside the trunk."

Liza squealed and covered her eyes. "It is a vampire and it's coming to get us!"

"It sounds to me more like whistling," Howie whispered.

"It's just the wind in this old attic," Eddie said. "C'mon. Let's find out what's in the trunk."

"Go ahead," Melody said.

Eddie shook his head. "You look."

"I'm not going to open it," Melody said.

"We'll count to three and look together,"

Howie interrupted. "One... two... THREE."

"Whew. It's just full of old clothes." Melody sighed as they opened the lid.

"Of course it is," Eddie said. "See? This is Uncle Jasper's old hat."

"That's the hat we saw in the window," Howie said slowly.

"Have you flipped?" Eddie said as he tried to put on the hat. "Hey! This won't fit."

"It's probably because your head is so big." Melody giggled.

"No, really. Look. Something's stuck under the lining," Eddie told them. He took off the hat and tugged at the material. It was so old it tore with very little pulling.

All the kids gulped when they saw what was inside the hat.

11

Hats Off to Uncle Jasper

"Wow!" Melody shrieked.

"There must be a million bucks in here," Eddie whistled as he thumbed through the wad of hundred dollar bills. "We're rich!"

"That's not OUR money," Melody told him. "It's Aunt Mathilda's."

"She doesn't even know it's here," Eddie snapped. "Uncle Jasper must have hidden it."

"It's still hers," Howie said firmly. "And she needs the money!"

"If you think I'm going to turn over all this dough to Aunt Mathilda, you've got bats in your belfry," Eddie told her.

Melody shook her finger at Eddie. "You're just as greedy as your Uncle Jasper."

"How can you even think of taking money from her? She may be in the hospital for weeks!" Liza said.

"Aw, I guess you're right," Eddie sighed. "But maybe she'll give us a reward."

"Eddie, you're hopeless." Melody started piling the money into an empty shoe box.

"We're lucky the light was on in the attic," Howie said. "Or we wouldn't have found the hat."

"It's almost as if someone wanted us to find it," Melody said slowly.

Liza nodded. "Jasper's ghost did. He had to help us find the money he hid from Aunt Mathilda so he could rest. If he were here we could thank him."

Eddie snickered. "Miss Manners herself, Emily P. Ghost!"

"Liza's right," Howie said slowly. "Maybe we should thank him."

Liza shook her head. "I don't think we'll find Uncle Jasper's ghost."

"Why not?" Howie asked.

Liza shrugged. "His wrong has been righted. He can rest now."

12

Coincidence?

Two months later, the four kids stared at Aunt Mathilda's house. "It looks great," Melody said.

"It is wonderful," Liza agreed. The old house didn't look the same. The roof was fixed and the windows were sparkling. New green paint covered the house and the shutters were a bright clean white.

The cheerful red door swung open and Aunt Mathilda waved at the four kids. She looked much better since coming home from the hospital. She wore jeans and a T-shirt, and her gray hair was tucked under a Bailey Elementary baseball cap.

"Don't just stand there," she bellowed. "Come in and let's play poker!"

Everyone laughed as they opened the new gate and walked up the steps.

"If it hadn't been for Jasper's hat, this house would've collapsed with the first snowflake," Melody laughed.

"It was lucky we found it," Howie said.

"That wasn't luck," Liza said quietly. "Jasper's ghost helped us find it."

"Naw, it was just dumb luck," Eddie said.

"I guess you're right," Melody admitted. "It was silly to think he could've been a ghost."

Howie laughed. "After all, ghosts don't eat potato chips!"

LITTLE 🍎 APPLE®

BABY-SITTERS

Little Sister®

by Ann M. Martin, author of *The Baby-sitters Club* ®

☐ MQ44300-3	#1	Karen's Witch	$2.75
☐ MQ44259-7	#2	Karen's Roller Skates	$2.75
☐ MQ44299-7	#3	Karen's Worst Day	$2.75
☐ MQ44264-3	#4	Karen's Kittycat Club	$2.75
☐ MQ44258-9	#5	Karen's School Picture	$2.75
☐ MQ43651-1	#10	Karen's Grandmothers	$2.75
☐ MQ43650-3	#11	Karen's Prize	$2.75
☐ MQ43649-X	#12	Karen's Ghost	$2.75
☐ MQ43648-1	#13	Karen's Surprise	$2.75
☐ MQ43646-5	#14	Karen's New Year	$2.75
☐ MQ43645-7	#15	Karen's In Love	$2.75
☐ MQ43644-9	#16	Karen's Goldfish	$2.75
☐ MQ43643-0	#17	Karen's Brothers	$2.75
☐ MQ43642-2	#18	Karen's Home-Run	$2.75
☐ MQ43641-4	#19	Karen's Good-Bye	$2.95
☐ MQ44823-4	#20	Karen's Carnival	$2.75
☐ MQ44824-2	#21	Karen's New Teacher	$2.95
☐ MQ44833-1	#22	Karen's Little Witch	$2.95
☐ MQ44832-3	#23	Karen's Doll	$2.95
☐ MQ44859-5	#24	Karen's School Trip	$2.75
☐ MQ44831-5	#25	Karen's Pen Pal	$2.75
☐ MQ44830-7	#26	Karen's Ducklings	$2.75
☐ MQ44829-3	#27	Karen's Big Joke	$2.75
☐ MQ44828-5	#28	Karen's Tea Party	$2.75
☐ MQ44825-0	#29	Karen's Cartwheel	$2.75
☐ MQ45645-8	#30	Karen's Kittens	$2.75
☐ MQ45646-6	#31	Karen's Bully	$2.95
☐ MQ45647-4	#32	Karen's Pumpkin Patch	$2.95
☐ MQ45648-2	#33	Karen's Secret	$2.95
☐ MQ45650-4	#34	Karen's Snow Day	$2.95
☐ MQ45652-0	#35	Karen's Doll Hosital	$2.95

Available wherever you buy books, or use this order form.

Scholastic Inc., P.O. Box 7502, 2931 E. McCarty Street, Jefferson City, MO 65102

Please send me the books I have checked above. I am enclosing $_____
(please add $2.00 to cover shipping and handling). Send check or money order - no cash
or C.O.Ds please.

Name _____

Address_____

City_____ State/Zip_____

Tell us your birth date! _____

BLS792